Puffin Books

DUMBELLINA

When her mum announces that th
Rebecca feels really miserable, unt

Dumbellina is a different sort of fairy. She doesn't wear frilly
dresses, and she is definitely not dainty – she's an iron fairy,
a tough-nut Tinkerbell, who won't stand for any nonsense
and has her own dynamic approach to solving Rebecca's
problems at her new school!

This is the sort of story that all young readers will enjoy.

Brough Girling was born in 1946. His previous jobs include
teacher, ice-cream salesman, business man, freelance copy
writer and promotions consultant. As well as writing
children's books he is Campaign Director of Readathon, the
sponsored reading event that raises money for the Malcolm
Sargent Cancer Fund for Children, and is Head of The
Children's Book Foundation at Book Trust in London.

Other books by Brough Girling

THE BANGERS AND CHIPS EXPLOSION
THE GREAT PUFFIN JOKE DIRECTORY
VERA PRATT AND THE BALD HEAD
VERA PRATT AND THE BISHOP'S FALSE TEETH
VERA PRATT AND THE FALSE MOUSTACHES

BROUGH GIRLING

DUMBELLINA

ILLUSTRATED BY CAROLINE SHARPE

PUFFIN BOOKS

PUFFIN BOOKS

Published by the Penguin Group
27 Wrights Lane, London W8 5TZ, England
Viking Penguin Inc., 40 West 23rd Street, New York, New York 10010, USA
Penguin Books Australia Ltd, Ringwood, Victoria, Australia
Penguin Books Canada Ltd, 2801 John Street, Markham, Ontario, Canada L3R 1B4
Penguin Books (NZ) Ltd, 182–190 Wairau Road, Auckland 10, New Zealand

Penguin Books Ltd, Registered Offices: Harmondsworth, Middlesex, England

First published by Viking Kestrel 1988
Published in Puffin Books 1990

Text copyright © Brough Girling, 1988
Illustrations copyright © Caroline Sharpe, 1988
All rights reserved

Made and printed in Great Britain by
Richard Clay Ltd, Bungay, Suffolk
Filmset in Palatino (Linotron 202)

CONTENTS

1.   Rebecca Baker

Mrs Baker, aged about thirty, was driving
her car home. Rebecca Baker, aged eight,
was sitting on the back seat behind her.
They had just finished doing some
shopping, and the front seat was full of
bags of groceries.

Rebecca was looking out of the window
and wasn't thinking about very much,
when her mother suddenly said: 'You know
I told you we were thinking about moving.
Well, I've got some really exciting news. We
are going to move. Graham's got a new job.
It's going to be a long way away so it will
mean a new house, and new schools for
you and Billy.'

Exciting news! It sounded more like

terrible news to Becca and a lumpy feeling came into her throat. She tried to swallow it.

She didn't want to know, or hear, any more. She felt her heart beat very fast, and she knew she couldn't speak. Ever since her mother had first mentioned they might be moving, she had dreaded that it might really happen. She couldn't stop her mother saying more – though she wanted to.

'You will still have a bedroom of your own. Graham and I have already decided which room will be yours, and it's very nice. So is the new house; and I'm sure you'll like the school. It's got a bigger field than St Bernard's, and you'll soon make new friends.'

Becca wanted the day to stop. She wanted her mother to be quiet, she wanted the car to stop and the road to open up and

swallow her. She felt that life as she knew it
was coming to an end.

It was the end of the world for Becca
Baker.

'All right, Rebecca?' said her mother, in a
slightly firm voice.

'No,' said Becca in a whisper. 'Not all right.'

'Oh, come on, darling! Lots of children have to move house, it won't be that bad. You'll soon get used to it.'

Becca's mind was spinning. She felt sick and stunned and silent. With a frozen gaze she stared at the back of the front seat.

Just then a large roaring lorry pulled out from a side-street in front of the car!

Becca's mother slammed on the brake. The car dipped down at the front and the tyres squealed. The shopping bags flew forwards off the front seat. Rebecca was thrown sideways and bumped her forehead against the window.

'OH BLAST!' shouted her mother.

The lorry roared off up the street, as Mrs Baker pulled into the side of the road.

Becca clasped her head with both hands, and looked at the back of the lorry as it disappeared up the road.

She saw that it wasn't a lorry at all. It was a small mobile crane. It had four large wheels and a cab at the front, and the long arm of the crane sat on big hydraulic legs along the top of it.

As it pounded its way into the distance, Becca could see that it had a name in large letters marked on the back of it, which said IRON FAIRY.

'Are you all right, Becca?' asked her mother, looking at her in the car's rear-view mirror.

'No,' said Becca, but she said it so quietly that no one could have heard her.

Her head hurt where she had bumped it, but it didn't hurt as much as the news that she would have to go to a new house, and a new school, and leave all the things she knew and liked.

She sank back into the hard car seat. Too stunned to cry, she stared silently through her fingers at the unfriendly world as they went home.

It was the worst day of her life.

2. *Home*

When Mrs Baker had parked the car in the front drive, she went round to the passenger door and organized the bags and packages that had fallen on to the floor of the car. She packed the groceries back into her shopping bag and put the carrier bags the right way up again.

She looked cross.

'Come on, Becca, love, out you get, and help me get these things into the kitchen.'

She looked over into the back of the car. Becca was silent, and motionless, with her hands still clasped to her forehead.

'Come on, darling,' said her mother, more kindly. 'It's not that bad!'

Becca didn't know what her mother

thought wasn't 'that bad'. To Becca everything seemed to be bad. Very bad indeed.

'Come on, then,' Mrs Baker repeated. 'Let's get you inside and have a look at that head of yours.'

They went inside. Billy Baker, Rebecca's elder brother, was sitting in the kitchen trying to teach the cat to talk: 'Who's a pretty boy then? Who's a pretty boy then?' he was saying.

'Come on, Billy, out of the way!' said his mother. 'We've just had a nasty mishap and Becca's bumped her head.'

'Trust Becca!' said her brother; not a very pleasant thing to say.

'Oh, go upstairs and tidy your room or something,' said Mrs Baker.

'OK, I'm going! Come on then, Bonzo,' he said to the cat, 'who's a pretty boy then?' And he and Bonzo left the room.

Becca sat on a stool.

'Now then, let's have a look,' said her
mother. She gently lifted Becca's hands
away from her forehead. 'Nothing to worry
about, but you're going to have quite a
bruise!'

Mrs Baker was right. There was a small, round, red lump where Becca's head had bumped against the window.

'Does it hurt?'

'Yes,' said Becca, but she didn't tell her mother that the thought of having to go to a new school, and a new house, hurt much more.

'Right. Let's get you up to bed for a bit of a rest. I'll bring you a cup of tea and a biscuit. Come on, off we go!'

She guided Becca up the stairs and into her small bedroom where she got under her bedcovers. Then her mother went down to put the kettle on.

Rebecca lay on her side and stared with wide open eyes at the wallpaper. It had swirly patterns on it and she was familiar with every inch of it. There was a bit near her pillow which looked like an elephant with its trunk in the air, and higher up it looked like the sun coming out from behind a cloud.

Her head seemed to be filled with a ringing sound and she could feel her pulse beating in her ears. The room was very silent, and she felt alone.

Quite suddenly her throat went lumpy again and hot tears filled her eyes. They ran, salty, down on to her pillow.

When Mrs Baker returned to the bedroom Becca was fast asleep. She put a mug of tea on the bedside table, anyway, and felt her daughter's forehead. It was warm, and damp. She pulled the covers up round Becca's small shoulders and went downstairs to have a word with Doctor Jenkins on the telephone.

When, a few hours later, Rebecca Baker woke up, night had fallen. The room was quite dark, except for the yellow light that came in through the window from the

lamppost outside the house. Usually Becca
would have closed her curtains to shut it
out.

She thought she heard a noise. It
sounded like a small, high clang – like
someone dropping a teaspoon on a hard
kitchen floor.

She heard it again. She sat up and peered
into the darkness round the bed.

Then she saw it.

On her bedside table stood a very small person. It appeared to be dressed in miniature dungarees, and in its two tiny hands it held a bright metal wand, with a star on top of it. It was swinging this with all its might against the cold mug of tea that Mrs Baker had left there, a bit like the man who beats that huge gong at the start of films.

'What . . . are . . . you?' asked Becca in a whisper.

'ME?' said the tiny creature, putting its hands on its hips for a moment. 'Why – I'm an IRON FAIRY!'

3. Becca's Iron Fairy

'Pardon?' said Becca, quietly.

'I said "I'm an Iron Fairy!" How do you do?'

'You don't *look* much like a fairy,' said Becca.

She was right: as her eyes grew accustomed to the dim light she could see the tiny creature in more detail. She was dressed, as Becca had first thought, in blue denim dungarees. Underneath these she seemed to have a check-shirt, and on her feet were a tiny pair of boots with bright steel toecaps – like someone working on a farm might wear. She had a red safety helmet on her head and looked more like a miniature road repairer than a fairy.

'Well!' said the Iron Fairy, '*I'm not like usual fairies*. I don't go prancing about all over the place, dangling from daisies and dancing about in soppy old daffodils! I'm TOUGH!'

'What do you do, then?' asked Becca.

'I sort things out!' Once more the small creature put her hands on her dungareed hips, and looked very determined.

'Do you do spells?' asked Becca again.

'Well, not exactly spells – but, boy-oh-boy, I can really make things happen!' She threw back her head in a confident laugh. 'You see,' she went on, 'I'm an all-action fairy. I don't flit about like some blooming butterfly. I've got better things to do. Get up and get at 'em, I say.'

24

Rebecca could not believe her eyes, or ears!

She noticed that the fairy looked a bit overweight. 'Although you're very small, you look sort of fat for an active fairy,' she said.

'Watch it, Mortal!' the Iron Fairy said sternly. 'I may look like a podge, but underneath these dungies I'm solid muscle. Iron muscle and nerves of steel, that's me! No messing!'

'And what are you doing here?'

'I've come to visit you, Kiddo! I reckon you've had rather a bad day. I can sense these things – all Iron Fairies can!'

For the first time since waking Becca was aware of a nasty tight feeling around her bruised forehead, and she remembered the events of the day before.

'I don't like to hear about children who fret and worry about this and that,' the fairy went on, 'so I've come to sort you out. We'll have you as right as rain in no time! No messing!'

She took another swing with her wand at the mug, making it clang and sending rings of ripples across the surface of the cold tea. 'This wand is stainless steel and as sharp as needles, and very good for getting people going, especially when I poke 'em with it!' The Iron Fairy laughed again, and Becca smiled for the first time in a long while.

'Do you have a name?' she asked.

'You bet I have a name! I'm called Dumbellina. DUMBELLINA THE IRON FAIRY!'

4.   *The Next Morning*

When Becca Baker woke up the next morning, the first thing she did was to look carefully at her bedside table.

The mug of stone-cold tea was there all right, but there was no sign of Dumbellina the Iron Fairy. Becca wondered if it had all been a dream: I expect you may be wondering the same thing.

She got out of bed and looked at herself in the mirror on the front of the wardrobe door. The swelling on her forehead had gone down a bit, but it was still there.

Her stepfather must have heard her moving about because he came into her room.

'Hi, Becca, how are you? Mum told me

you got a nasty bump when she nearly got hit by that lorry.'

'It wasn't a lorry, Graham, it was an Iron Fairy,' said Becca.

'What on earth's an Iron Fairy?'

'It's a sort of crane, on wheels,' said Becca.

'Well, are you OK now? Let me look at that head of yours.'

He examined her forehead. 'It doesn't look too bad. Doctor Jenkins said that as long as you feel fit today you can go to school as usual. All right?'

'Yes,' said Becca.

'Good girl, come and have some breakfast when you're dressed.'

He went out and shut the door.

Rebecca got dressed for school, and as she did so the fears and worries about moving house and school began to fill her head again. She went down to the kitchen for breakfast, and sat down between her mum and Graham.

He put a bowl of cornflakes down in front of her. 'Mum says she thinks you're a bit upset about us having to move,' he said in a gentle voice.

'Yes,' said Becca, and she looked hard at the cornflakes and tried not to start crying.

'Well, it won't be so bad. You'll like the

new house, and the school looks very nice.'

Becca sniffed, and she thought. She thought about her friends. She knew she didn't want to know any more about moving.

Then she thought about Bonzo the cat.

'What are you so worried about, dear?' she heard her mother's voice asking.

'Bonzo won't want to move,' said Becca.

'Oh, come off it, Becca! He won't mind moving. Now don't be a silly girl. Off you go to school.'

Suddenly Rebecca did not want to go to school. She hated the idea: she wanted to sulk. She wanted to do *anything* that would stop her mum and Graham making this terrible move.

She sat for a moment and stared at her cornflake bowl. Then she felt a sharp pain in her left leg, down by her ankle. She looked down, ready to scratch it.

There, on the floor near her shoe, stood Dumbellina!

She was looking very determined, and was jabbing Becca's ankle with the needle-sharp tip of her spiky little stainless-steel wand!

'Oi, Mortal!' she said. 'Come on! Stop that fretting and get off to school. Sulking never did anyone any good – it's the sort of thing soppy little girls in ghastly party frocks do!'

Becca's mouth opened in amazement. She managed not to speak, and because her mother and Graham were clearing away the breakfast things, she thought they had probably not noticed anything.

But now Rebecca Baker knew two things for certain: Dumbellina the Iron Fairy had not been a dream, and she was going to have to face the day at school after all!

5. At School

In the first lesson after morning assembly
Miss Wrigley said they would have 'News'.
Miss Wrigley's class did 'News' nearly
every week.

She would ask children in the class if they
had any news, and then, if they did, she
would write the news up on the blackboard
with the child's name beside it. The class
news would then stay on the board all
morning.

Becca didn't often have any news, and
she was usually shy about it when she did.
She was always frightened that people
would laugh at what she said. Other
children, like her friend Dan, always had
lots and lots of news.

This morning Becca felt different. This might be her big moment: she would never dare tell the class about Dumbellina, but she could tell everyone the sad news about her move.

'Who has got some news today?' asked Miss Wrigley.

'I have, Miss!' said Dan.

'We'll come to you in a minute, Dan, let someone else have a turn first.'

Richard Matthews said that his gran was coming at the weekend. Miss Wrigley wrote it on the board.

Becca put up her hand.

'Yes, Rebecca?' said Miss Wrigley.

'Please, Miss Wrigley,' said Becca quietly. 'I'm going to leave this school.'

'Don't be silly, Rebecca,' said Miss Wrigley, and turned to Jennifer Jones who had her hand up.

Becca could not believe it! Why wasn't

Miss Wrigley writing up her stunning piece of sad news? Why was she going on to Jennifer Jones's news and not writing *hers* up!

Jennifer Jones said that her gerbil had died in the night. Miss Wrigley wrote it up on the blackboard. Jennifer Jones looked very pleased.

Becca stared at Miss Wrigley with all her might, but she was too scared to put her hand up again, or to say what she was feeling.

Tears were coming into Becca's eyes, and she wiped them away with her forearm. Then an amazing thing happened. When she looked up to the front of the room, Dumbellina the Iron Fairy was standing on Miss Wrigley's shoulder!

She was standing there as plain as plain could be! Even from three rows back Becca could see Dumbellina's determined little face, her blue dungarees and her stout, steel-capped boots.

The extraordinary thing was that none of the other children in the class seemed to be able to see anything strange. They were all getting on in the usual way.

Rebecca watched, spellbound.

Dumbellina was holding her wand with both hands and was reaching upwards with it. Then she poked it in Miss Wrigley's ear!

Miss Wrigley seemed to feel it all right, because she jumped in the air with a little yelp and waved at her ear as if a wasp had landed on it.

For an awful moment Becca thought that the Iron Fairy would get squashed, and she shot up her hand and called loudly: 'Please, Miss!'

'What is it, Rebecca?'

'Please . . . Miss . . .' repeated Becca slowly. 'Please . . .'

She stopped speaking. There was no way

she could tell Miss Wrigley to be careful of the Iron Fairy on her shoulder! How the class would laugh at her.

However, Dumbellina was not on Miss Wrigley's shoulder any more. She seemed to have disappeared.

Becca started to turn very red, and had just begun to put her hand down and get ready to be told off by Miss Wrigley, when Dumbellina appeared in the middle of Becca's desk. She popped out from behind Becca's pencil-case and looked her straight in the eye.

'Go on!' said the Iron Fairy very firmly. 'Tell her to put *your* news up on the board, or I'll go and sort her out with my needle-sharp, stainless-steel wand!'

'Well, Rebecca, what is it?' Miss Wrigley was saying.

'I *am* leaving this school please, Miss Wrigley,' said Rebecca Baker.

'That's the way!' whispered Dumbellina.

'My stepdad has got a new job and we are
going to move . . . Please would you put
my news on the board,' she added bravely.

'I'm sorry, Becca, you didn't explain
yourself properly. I thought you were just
being silly. Yes, of course I will.' And Miss
Wrigley turned her back on the class and
began writing Becca's news on the
blackboard.

Dumbellina started running round on the
top of Becca's desk like a footballer who's
just scored a very important goal. None of
the other children seemed able to see her. It
was amazing!

'Well done, Kiddo!' shouted Dumbellina,
punching her arms in the air. 'That showed
her! No messing! That sorted the old girl
out, and no mistake.'

And the next moment the Iron Fairy had
gone!

6.   *That Night*

Back in her bedroom that night Becca couldn't sleep.

Half of her was excited about the help she'd had from Dumbellina, and the other half was worrying about having to go to a new school.

Then she heard a voice she knew.

'Come on, Mortal! Stop messing about with all those worries!'

There was Dumbellina, with her sparkling wand in her hand, standing on her bedside table.

'Hallo, Dumbellina,' said Becca.

'Watcha, Kiddo,' said the fairy.

'How is it, Dumbellina, that other people can't see you, and I can?' asked Becca.

'Oh, that's easy. I'm on a special mission to help you. I'm your very own fairy trouble-shooter, so only you can see me! Iron Fairies are up to all sorts of tricks like that. If *everyone* could see us it would give the game away!'

'What's a trouble-shooter?'

'Well, if you've got trouble in your way, I shoot it *out* of your way – simple! Like the way we dealt with silly old Miss Wrigleybottom this morning!'

'Hey, you're not supposed to call her that!' said Becca Baker, rather surprised.

'Why not?' said Dumbellina. 'It suits her!'

'I never knew that fairies called people rude names,' said Becca.

'Most fairies don't, but Iron Fairies are a different matter. We're solid muscle, and we care for no one! We don't dress up in ghastly pink ballet dresses, or mess about in flower petals or play about with moonbeams or dewdrops or thistle-down. When we've got a job to do we do it, and if we get the chance to lark about a bit at the same time, we take it! . . . Now then, why aren't you fast asleep, you frightful little mortal?'

'I can't sleep, Dumbellina, because I'm feeling too sad.'

'Now then, don't get all drippy! What are you sad about?'

'Mum says I've only got one more week at St Bernard's, and then we are going to move. I shall never see my friends again!'

'Well,' said Dumbellina thoughtfully, 'I can see that that is quite sad. I'm sure you are right: there will be lots of friends of yours at St Bernard's that you won't see again – but when something sad comes along it's much better to take it on the chin, like I do, than droop about like a hen that's wet its knickers!'

They both laughed at this.

'And look on the bright side,' went on Dumbellina. 'You will go to a new school the week after next, and it will have a whole lot of *new* friends for you in it!'

45

The mention of the new school made Becca look a bit downcast again.

'Have you got any really *special* friends at St Bernard's?' asked Dumbellina.

'Oh, yes!' said Becca, 'there's Sally and Dan for a start!'

'Well, I think you should tell them that you know you will miss them, and ask them to write to you. Turn them into pen-friends – no problem! You never lose good friends if you work at it! Good-night.'

And once more she was gone.

7. Bonzo Baker

'But what about Bonzo?' said Becca firmly.

As you probably remember, Bonzo was the Baker family's cat. He was ginger and lazy, with white under his chin.

It was the morning of the house move. The family had all had breakfast in the bare kitchen, and most of the chests and boxes and furniture were now in the back of the huge van that Graham had rented for the move.

'What do you mean, dear, "what about Bonzo?"' asked Mrs Baker.

'Well, how are we going to move him? He'll hate it!'

'I've told you before, Rebecca, he'll be OK. I've got the cat basket ready for him –

he's so sleepy these days that he probably won't even notice what is going on,' said Becca's mother.

She was wrong. Cats *always* know what's going on, and Bonzo had been watching the packing very carefully. When Becca got up from the table and began to look for him, she couldn't find him anywhere!

She went through all the rooms. It made her feel strange: they were empty and bare and echoing, and not like home at all. 'Bonzo! Bonzo! Come on, boy!' she called, but no ginger cat appeared.

When she went back to the kitchen Graham came in through the back door. He had been outside putting his garden things into the back of the van.

'You'll never guess what!' he said. 'I've just seen where Bonzo is. He's in the front garden. He's stuck half-way up the walnut tree! That's *all* we need!'

Rebecca, her brother Billy, and her

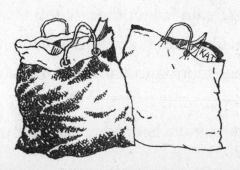

mother and Graham all went out into the front garden. There, out on the end of a thin branch, was Bonzo Baker.

He was looking down at them, miaowing.

'I know what it is!' said Becca. 'He doesn't want to move house. I don't blame him!' Tears began to come into her eyes.

'Oh, come off it, Rebecca,' said Graham.

'How on earth are you going to get him down, though?' Mrs Baker asked him. 'We're supposed to be out of here in half an hour – the next people's van will arrive any minute. What *are* we going to do?'

'I might be able to shift him with my catapult,' said Billy, trying to be helpful.

'BILLY!' said his mother. 'I don't want to hear talk like that! Poor Bonzo. Any more silly suggestions and you will go straight up to your bedroom!'

'I haven't got a bedroom!' said Billy. 'If

only I'd been able to teach him how to talk –
I could have a conversation with him and
he could tell us what was up.'

'We *know* what's up, Billy, Bonzo is up
. . . in the tree!' said Graham.

They all looked up at the branches of the
walnut tree again. Suddenly it looked as if
Bonzo might start coming down of his own
accord! He had turned to face the trunk,
and was making very slow and careful
progress along the branch towards it.

'Look!' cried Mrs Baker. 'He's trying to
come down. I wonder why he's being so
helpful all of a sudden!'

Only Rebecca could see the answer. She could see that Bonzo was being pushed from behind by a very determined Iron Fairy!

Dumbellina was right behind Bonzo. She was leaning hard on the back of his hind legs, and every now and again she was prodding his furry bottom with her steel wand. She was working extremely hard!

'Come on, you stupid great cat! Down you go! No messing! Surely you can climb down a tree better than this. I thought *I* was overweight! Stop going so gingerly.'

'Don't be daft, Fairy,' said Bonzo. 'After all, I am a ginger cat!'

'Cut the jokes, Puss, and get going!' said Dumbellina, poking his bottom with the wand again.

'Well, you stop doing that then!' said Bonzo. He was not amused, but he was moving.

Dumbellina the Iron Fairy had come to the rescue, and half an hour later the Baker family were on their way to a new home. Graham went ahead in the van, and Mrs Baker followed with Billy and Becca , and Bonzo, in the car.

8.   The New Home

The main thing about the new house was that Becca instantly liked it!

It had a small gravel drive at the front of it and a flower-bed full of roses. It looked friendly.

'Cor . . .' said Becca.

Her mother parked the car in the gateway behind the hired van, and Becca and Billy got out. The gravel was crunchy under their feet – like walking on a stony beach.

'Follow me then, kids, I'll show you your new rooms.' They followed her through the front door.

Graham was already carrying things into the house, so they had to squeeze past several big tea chests before climbing the stairs.

Becca's room was lovely. It had a big window that looked down into the garden, and was larger and brighter than the little bedroom she'd left behind. Graham and Billy brought her bed upstairs. They put it in the middle of the bare room.

'Here you are, Becca. I shouldn't start sorting out where you are going to put things until we've got your table and wardrobe and other bits in.'

Becca sat down on the bed, alone in the empty room. She was smiling. Suddenly there was a sharp tap on the window. She looked up and there stood Dumbellina. She had her wand in one hand and she was rapping on the glass with it. Becca got up and opened the window.

'Hi there, Kiddo!'

'Hallo, Dumbellina – this is my new room!'

'I know *that*!' said the Iron Fairy. 'A bit of all right, isn't it?'

'Yes, I like it. I didn't think I'd ever have a room as nice as my old one.'

'Look, Becca,' said Dumbellina, taking off her workman's helmet and folding her arms. 'Didn't you hear Graham and your mum both telling you that you'd be moving to a nicer house? That's typical of you – you were worrying about nothing! Worrying never did anyone any good, so stop messing!'

'Yes,' said Becca quietly, 'but I am still a bit worried about going to my new school on Monday.'

'Well, I suppose that's not too surprising – but I'll be around if anyone needs sorting out! You'll be amazed what a prod up the backside with a bit of stainless steel can do to get people going! Just ask your cat Bonzo!'

Becca smiled again.

'Well, I must be off,' said Dumbellina, wiping her forehead with a grubby-looking handkerchief and putting her helmet back on. 'I've got some other kids to sort out, you know – an Iron Fairy's job is never done!'

In a trice she was gone.

The family spent the rest of the day unloading the van, and beginning to get their new home into some kind of order. Becca and Billy also explored the garden, and went down to look at the local shops. Bonzo spent several hours sniffing the skirting boards, and then went to sleep in a cardboard box.

They had tea in the kitchen surrounded by boxes and newspaper.

'An early bed for you two,' said Graham to Billy and Becca when tea was over. He was feeling very tired.

'I say, Rebecca, you've still got quite a mark on your forehead, haven't you?' said Mrs Baker.

'That's her Iron Fairy bruise!' said Graham with a smile.

Becca felt it with her hand. Yes, it still felt a bit tender.

9.   The New School

After breakfast the next Monday morning Mrs Baker put Billy and Becca into the car and took them to St Gertrude's – their new school.

Becca was feeling very nervous. She spent the journey fiddling with her school-bag, and checking that she had her dinner money, pencil-case and dictionary.

She took the pencil-case out of the bag and unzipped it to make sure that she had her felt-tip pens. They were there all right, and so was Dumbellina!

She was fast asleep at the bottom of the case, among some pencil sharpenings, with her hands behind her head and her workman's helmet tipped forward over her

eyes. She looked like a tiny farmworker having a snooze in his lunch break.

Becca's mouth opened in surprise. Dumbellina woke up, pushed the brim of her helmet back with the tip of her wand and looked at her. 'Don't you fret, Kiddo!' she said. 'I'm here and ready for action.'

A moment later they had driven through the school gates and Mrs Baker was knocking on a door marked SCHOOL SECRETARY.

'Good morning,' said a very large lady. 'I'm Mrs Snapdragon, the School Secretary. Can I help you?'

'Yes,' said Mrs Baker, 'this is Billy and Rebecca Baker – they're starting today.'

'Ah yes, William will go to upper assembly and I'll take Rebecca down to lower assembly with me in a moment. There's another new girl starting this morning, so we'll all go together.'

The other new girl was called Sharma. After assembly Becca and Sharma were taken to their new classroom. The teacher told them to sit together.

Becca liked Sharma. She was a quiet, slightly shy girl rather like her: once or twice they smiled at one another when someone said something funny. It felt friendly.

They got on quite well all morning. It was not as bad as Becca had feared – the teacher was kind to them and the other children didn't take any special notice of her.

But when the dinner bell rang an unpleasant thing happened. As Becca went to stand up she felt as if someone was pulling her hair, and Sharma's chair made a scraping sound on the floor.

The two children behind them had tied their hair to the backs of their chairs!

10.   Rivers and Smith

In the dinner break Becca went off to a quiet corner of the playing field and opened her pencil-case. Sure enough, Dumbellina was still inside it. 'Do you know what happened?' she said.

'Yes!' said Dumbellina. 'Of *course* I do. I know *everything* – all Iron Fairies do!'

'Well, what should I do? I hate those two children and I'm scared what they will do to us next. I want to go home!'

'That wouldn't do a lot of good! What about poor Sharma! No, you've got to deal with this before it gets worse,' said Dumbellina, crossing her muscular arms across the bib of her dungarees. 'Sort the little rotters out! Tell them that you don't like that kind of behaviour, and even though they may be a bit bigger than you, you want them to know that you think they are cowards and bullies!'

'Golly!' said Becca. 'Have I got to say all that?'

'Too right, Chum! You've got *me* on your side now, you know, so stick up for yourself.'

During the first lesson after dinner Rebecca learnt the names of the two children who were sitting behind her. They were Paul Rivers and Jennifer Smith.

During the afternoon play she summoned up all her courage, put a frown on her face, clenched her fists and went striding up to them: 'Excuse me,' she said. It came out much too softly, so she said it again. 'Excuse me, but I don't think it was very kind of you to tie me and my friend Sharma's hair to our chairs on our first morning at school.'

'Huh!' said Paul Rivers. 'Just you wait for your *second* day at school. You ain't seen nothing yet!'

What a horrible boy! thought Becca, and it made her bolder. 'I think you are very horrible: how would you like it if someone bullied you!'

'No one would!' said Jennifer Smith. 'We rule this class, see! We're daredevils! Rivers and Smith – we go together like Starsky and Hutch! No one gets the better of us because we dare each other to do things all the time. He dared me to tie her hair to the chair and I dared him to tie yours. Simple!'

'Well, I don't call that very daring,' said Becca.

'What do *you* call daring, then?' asked Paul Rivers scornfully.

'I don't know – but not that.'

'If you think you're so brave we'll set *you* a dare,' said Jennifer Smith.

'Yeah!' scoffed Rivers. 'Bet you wouldn't come back after school tonight and let out all the school pets!'

'Of course I wouldn't, don't be so stupid!' Rebecca Baker turned on her heels and walked away from the silly children. As she did so she heard a small shrill voice in her ear saying: 'Well done, Kiddo! You stuck up for yourself like a star!'

'WELL, *WE* DARE!' she heard Jennifer Smith shout.

11.   After School

Billy and Becca walked home after school: it was not very far.

For the whole of the journey Becca's mind was in a whirl: was it really possible? Were Paul Rivers and Jennifer Smith going to let the school pets out that evening?

She longed to open her pencil-case to see if Dumbellina was still around, but she couldn't do that with Billy there – he'd think she was nutty!

When they got home Mrs Baker greeted them with news that made Becca feel a whole lot worse.

'Hallo, you two; how did you get on? Hurry up and have your tea because you are going to have to go out afterwards and look for Bonzo. He seems to have wandered off.'

'*You mean he's run away!*' said Becca. 'I *said* he didn't want to move house.' Tears welled up in her eyes.

'Now stop worrying, Rebecca, I'm sure we'll find him.'

Becca ate the sandwiches and cake her mother had put in the kitchen and gulped down a glass of milk. Then she grabbed her school-bag from the hall and ran up to her bedroom with it. 'Dumbellina will know where he's gone, she'll tell me what to do,' she said to herself as she crossed the landing.

She opened her bag and unzipped her pencil-case. Dumbellina wasn't there!

'Oh no!' said Becca out loud. 'Where's my Iron Fairy, just when I need her?'

There was a ring at the doorbell and Mrs Baker called up the stairs: 'Becca! It's someone for you.'

Becca went downstairs, and there on the doorstep stood Sharma. 'Hallo, Becca,' she said. 'Would you like to come round to my house to watch telly or something?'

'Well, actually our cat has just run away. I'm *very* worried because we've only been here for three days and he won't know his way around. You could help me look if you like.'

'All right,' said Sharma.

The two girls set off along the road and Becca described the cat to Sharma. They looked over walls and hedges into people's front gardens, and called 'Bonzo! Bonzo

Baker!' as they went. They didn't really take much notice of where they were going. They just followed their noses and concentrated on looking for Bonzo.

'There he is!' called Becca cheerfully, pointing to the bottom of a small hedge. But when the girls got closer they saw that it was only a brown paper bag.

There was a gap in the hedge where children had obviously ridden bicycles through it. On the other side was a large green field, but it wasn't until they had crossed through into it that they realized where they were. They were back at St Gertrude's, on the edge of the school playing field.

'I don't think he will have come this far, Sharma,' said Becca. 'He's very fat and lazy. I suppose we'd better go home and look down by the shops.'

Deep inside her Rebecca had one huge

fear: that Bonzo had been run over.

The late summer sun was just beginning to go down as the girls took one last look across the school playing field. When Becca's eyes scanned the school buildings she saw something that took her breath away!

12. Rivers and Smith Again!

Two children were climbing in through one of the school lavatory windows!

It was not very difficult for Becca to decide who they were. 'LOOK!' she called to Sharma. 'That's Paul Rivers and Jennifer Smith – the horrible children who sat behind us and tied our hair to the chairs – and they're breaking into the school! I think I know what they're up to!'

She told Sharma about the daredevil boasting and what they said they dared to do after school.

'Oh, Becca! What do you think we should do?' Sharma sounded very frightened.

Rebecca Baker didn't spend much time thinking about what she should do; instead she imagined how Dumbellina the Iron Fairy would answer that question. 'There's only one thing we *can* do, Sharma,' she said quietly, 'we'll go and sort them out . . . no messing.'

The two girls went round through the hedge again and approached the school along the road, so that neither Rivers nor Smith would see them crossing the field. They tiptoed in through the front gate, dodged by the bike sheds and ran round to the opened lavatory window.

When they got there Becca's heart sank. A little further along the building was the door the infants used to reach the playing field. It was open, and six rather bewildered white rabbits were lolloping about on the grass!

Bravely the girls slipped in through the open door.

The new school felt even more strange and unfamiliar with no one in it! It was silent, and chilly. Then they jumped: two shrieking budgerigars arrowed down a

corridor at them, and as they ducked down behind a bookcase Becca felt sure that she saw a hamster run across the front of her shoe.

'It's Paul Rivers and Jennifer Smith all right, and they're carrying out their dare!' whispered Becca. Sharma looked wide-eyed and alarmed.

Four guinea-pigs ran down the corridor and turned left into the infants room, like clockwork toys.

The girls both froze as they thought they heard the sound of Rivers' and Smith's voices coming down the corridor towards them!

'*I dare you to put the fish down the toilets!*' they heard Paul Rivers say, '*there's a tank full of them in 3A.*'

The girls looked around. They were standing right beside a classroom door: it had 3A on it in large red letters!

'They're coming this way! Quick, we'll hide in here!' whispered Becca urgently. They went into the classroom and hid behind the door.

Seventeen white mice scampered happily down the corridor and ran outside.

A moment later Paul Rivers and Jennifer Smith were in 3A too. They went straight over towards the teacher's desk, which had a large fish tank beside it.

Quick as a flash Becca and Sharma dashed from the room and Becca did a very intelligent thing. She shut the door and turned the key in the lock!

The door had a glass panel in it, and they could see the two children swing round from the fish tank with very surprised looks on their faces. Becca and Sharma knew that they had been seen. 'It's those new girls!' they heard Paul Rivers exclaim.

Seven gerbils scurried down the corridor and out into the open air.

'What are we going to do now, Becca?' cried Sharma with panic in her voice.

'I'll tell you what to do, Kiddo!' said a small shrill voice, and there was Dumbellina standing on top of a fire extinguisher.

'Where have you been, Dumbellina?' asked Becca.

'Oh . . . here and there, you know. It's a busy life in Iron Fairyland.'

'It's a busy life here as well!' said Becca, as two terrapins waddled past and went into the boys' lavatory.

'Why are you talking to that fire extinguisher, Becca?' asked Sharma, looking puzzled and even more frightened.

'Oh, I'll explain that later,' she replied. 'Whatever should we do, Dumbellina – those bullies will murder us!'

'No problem!' said Dumbellina. 'We'll raise the alarm!' She leapt up on to a square alarm-bell switch above the extinguisher. It had a small glass cover which said, 'In Case of Emergency Break Glass'. With one blow of her stainless-steel wand she smashed the glass cover, and the evening air filled with the sound of alarm bells ringing!

13. No Messing!

Rivers and Smith heard the bells ring, and they started to panic.

They tried all the windows in the classroom but found that they were firmly locked.

Mrs Snapdragon, in her house opposite the school gates, also heard the bells ring, and she put down her knitting. She stamped her large feet into some sensible shoes before striding over towards the school.

All the parents in the nearby houses heard the bells ring, and they put down their evening papers, or stopped ironing, or stopped digging, or stopped doing nothing, or whatever they were doing, and they all started heading for the school.

'Right!' said Dumbellina to Becca. 'Time for action. Let's get these animals sorted out, no messing! Off we go!'

Off they went.

The next surprise happened when Dumbellina ran out on to the playing field and leapt on to the ginger back of Bonzo Baker!

She charged off like a knight on horseback, with her needle-sharp wand held like a lance under one arm. Bonzo galloped at a furious pace towards the white rabbits, who were now peacefully grazing in the middle of the football pitch.

Becca was so relieved to see Bonzo safe

and sound, and she had certainly never ever seen him move so fast.

'Come on, Bonzo, my trusty steed!' said Dumbellina, reaching up to speak in the large cat's ear. 'Up and at them! Don't pussyfoot around!'

'Don't be daft, Fairy! I'm doing my best – after all, I have got pussy feet, you know!'

What Mrs Snapdragon and all the parents saw when they arrived on the scene was an overweight ginger cat rounding up rabbits, mice, hamsters, gerbils and guinea-pigs. It obviously wasn't attacking them; it was simply driving them all back towards the school door like a dog in a sheep-dog trial!

Mrs Snapdragon came up to Becca and Sharma, who were standing by the open door.

'Whatever is going on?' she asked them. 'Whose wonderful cat is that? And how did all these pets get out?'

'Please, he's my cat,' said Becca. 'He's called Bonzo, and the pets got out because two children got in and let them out. They're in 3A.'

This was not quite accurate. The two children *had* been in 3A, but now the room was empty!

The minute Mrs Snapdragon unlocked the door and went into 3A, she could see what had happened. Paul Rivers and

Jennifer Smith had put tables and chairs under the skylight and had climbed out on to the flat roof!

She went outside again. By this time all the parents were cheering as Bonzo Baker sped from one straying pet to the next. He'd turn a rabbit back towards the school, then sidestep as a gerbil tried to make a break for open space. He was magic!

Only Rebecca could see all the hard work Dumbellina was putting in, digging her steel-capped boots into the cat's sides, and prodding pets up the backside with her steel wand as she shot by them!

Soon all the pets were back in the school. Just as the assembled parents broke into a

spontaneous round of applause, and Mrs Snapdragon shut the door on the recaptured school pets, Paul Rivers and Jennifer Smith swung down from the guttering and landed right beside her!

14. *Goodbye Dumbellina*

Almost at the very moment when the two terrible children's feet touched the playground they started running, and almost at the moment when Mrs Snapdragon *saw* them running, she started to chase them!

She set off like a rhino that's been stung on the bum. The ground shook, Paul Rivers and Jennifer Smith yelled in terror, and the crowd of parents cheered. For a large School Secretary, Mrs Snapdragon moved extremely fast.

By the time she reached the edge of the football pitch she was nearly up to them, and by the time *they* reached the middle of it she was only a foot or so behind them.

Her sensible shoes pounded the ground like pistons, and her woolly cardigan billowed behind her like a banner. She was *very* impressive! How the parents cheered!

In another stride or two she made a brave and final move – she dived headlong at the two pairs of legs and brought off a unique and amazing double rugger tackle!

A cloud of dust rose into the evening air, and when it cleared the crowd could see that Mrs Snapdragon had a child tucked securely under each of her mighty arms.

Becca could see that Dumbellina was also part of the scene. She was busily tying

Rivers' and Smith's shoelaces together as an added precaution.

'Right!' said Mrs Snapdragon, walking over to the parents. 'I'm going to take a little walk with these two to see Mr and Mrs Rivers, and Mr and Mrs Smith. I shall then call at the Head Teacher's house and arrange for a special assembly tomorrow with the presentation of a prize to these brave two new girls and this remarkable cat, Bonzo Baker!'

Becca picked up the exhausted Bonzo and

then she and Sharma started to walk back to Becca's house.

They had not gone very far when Becca heard a voice she knew. 'Hi there, Kiddo!' it said, and there was Dumbellina doing pull-ups on a twig in the hedgerow beside them.

'Well!' she said, 'that was a bit of fun and no mistake! But I'm off now – I've got a lot of other little worriers to sort out! Bye. Be seeing you!'

And Dumbellina disappeared.

Rebecca Baker was not really sure what Dumbellina meant by 'Be seeing you', but she rather feared that she would not see her Iron Fairy again. This made her feel a bit sad, but she also knew that thanks to Dumbellina she was now part of her new school, and she was able to look forward to the next day's assembly with a warm feeling.

'Goodbye, Dumbellina,' she said to the thin evening air.

When she got home Mrs Baker was
pleased to see her, and to see Bonzo. 'Well
done, Becca! You've found him!' she said.

'Yes, we found him, and we had an
adventure or two at the same time,' replied
Becca.

'You do look *very* tired – are you all right?
How's that bruise of yours?'

Rebecca put her hand up to her forehead
to check. The Iron Fairy bruise had
disappeared completely.